Mighty Mighty MONSTERS

SCIENCE FAIR
NIGHTMARE

created by
Sean O'Reilly

illustrated by
Arcana Studio

In a strange corner of the world known as Transylmania . . .

Legendary monsters were born.

WELCOME TO TRANSYLMANIA

But long before their frightful fame, these classic creatures faced fears of their own.

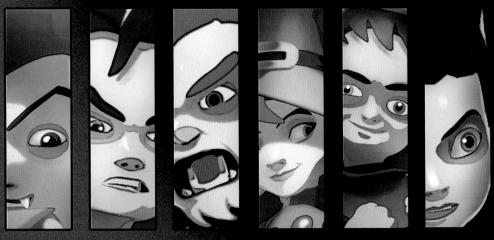

To take on terrifying teachers and homework horrors,
they formed the most fearsome friendship on Earth . . .

Mighty Mighty MONSTERS

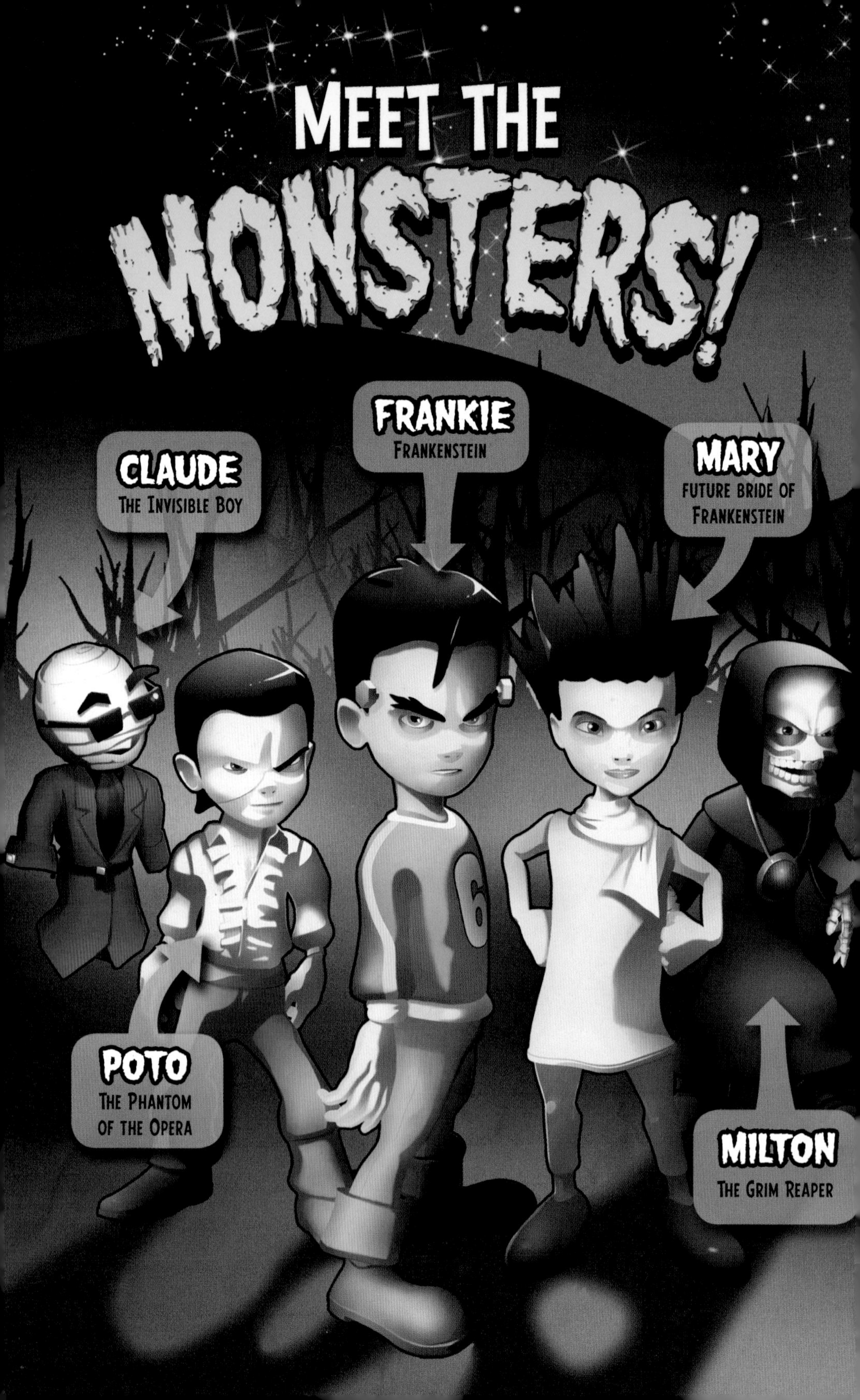
MEET THE
MONSTERS!
CLAUDE
THE INVISIBLE BOY
FRANKIE
FRANKENSTEIN
MARY
FUTURE BRIDE OF FRANKENSTEIN
POTO
THE PHANTOM OF THE OPERA
MILTON
THE GRIM REAPER

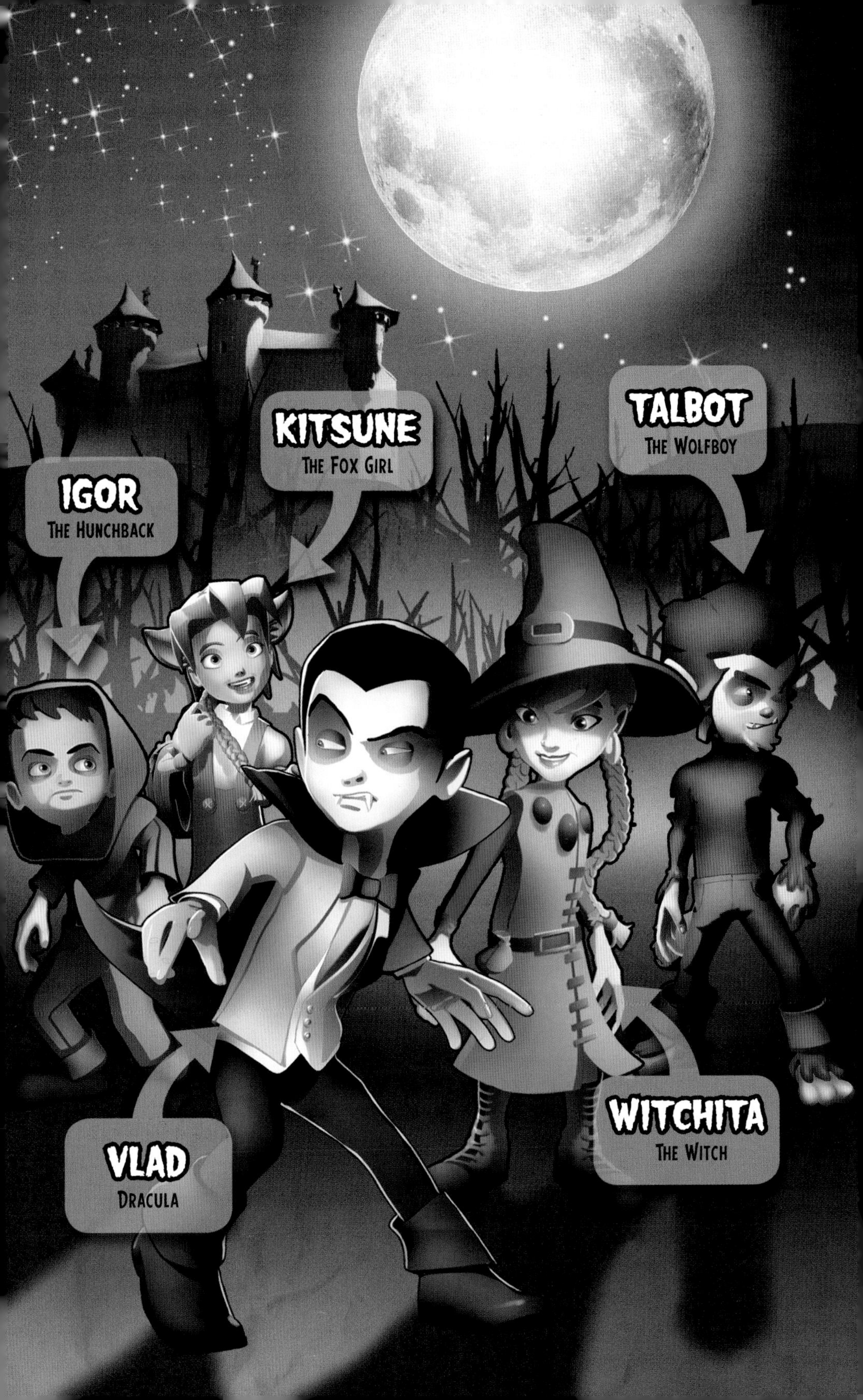
KITSUNE
THE FOX GIRL
TALBOT
THE WOLFBOY
IGOR
THE HUNCHBACK
VLAD
DRACULA
WITCHITA
THE WITCH

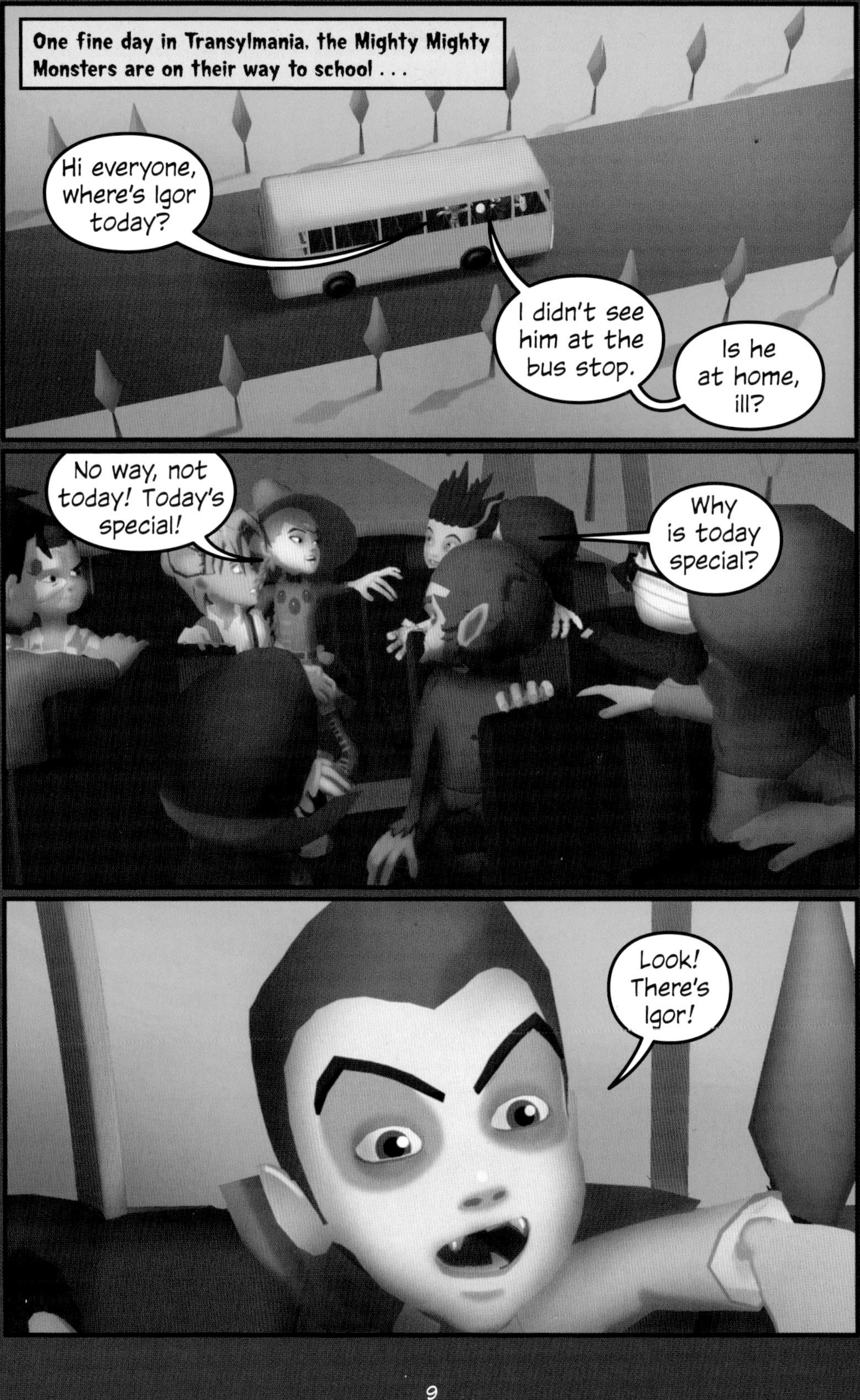

One fine day in Transylmania, the Mighty Mighty Monsters are on their way to school . . .
Hi everyone, where's Igor today?
I didn't see him at the bus stop.
Is he at home, ill?
No way, not today! Today's special!
Why is today special?
Look! There's Igor!

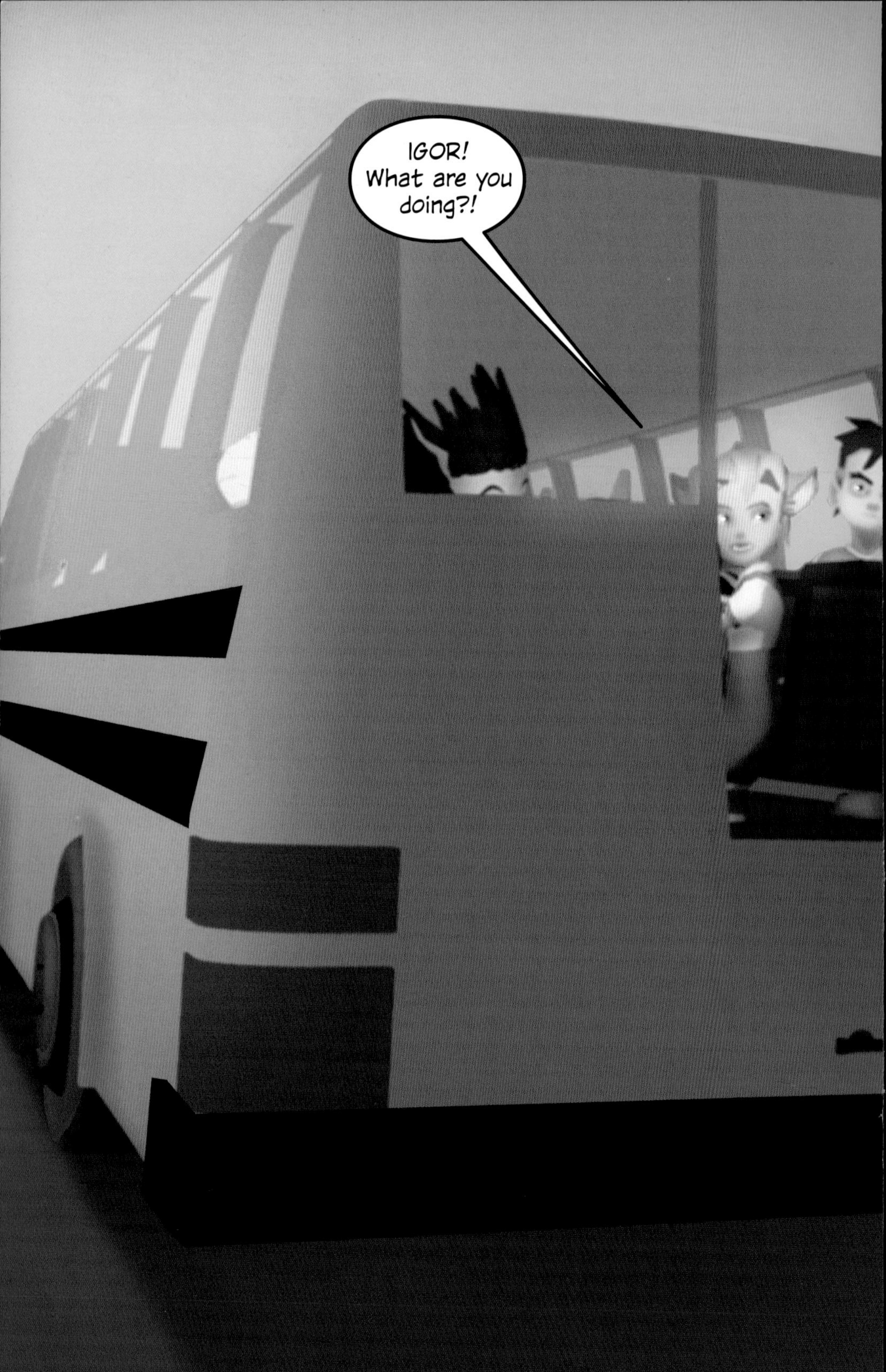
IGOR! What are you doing?!

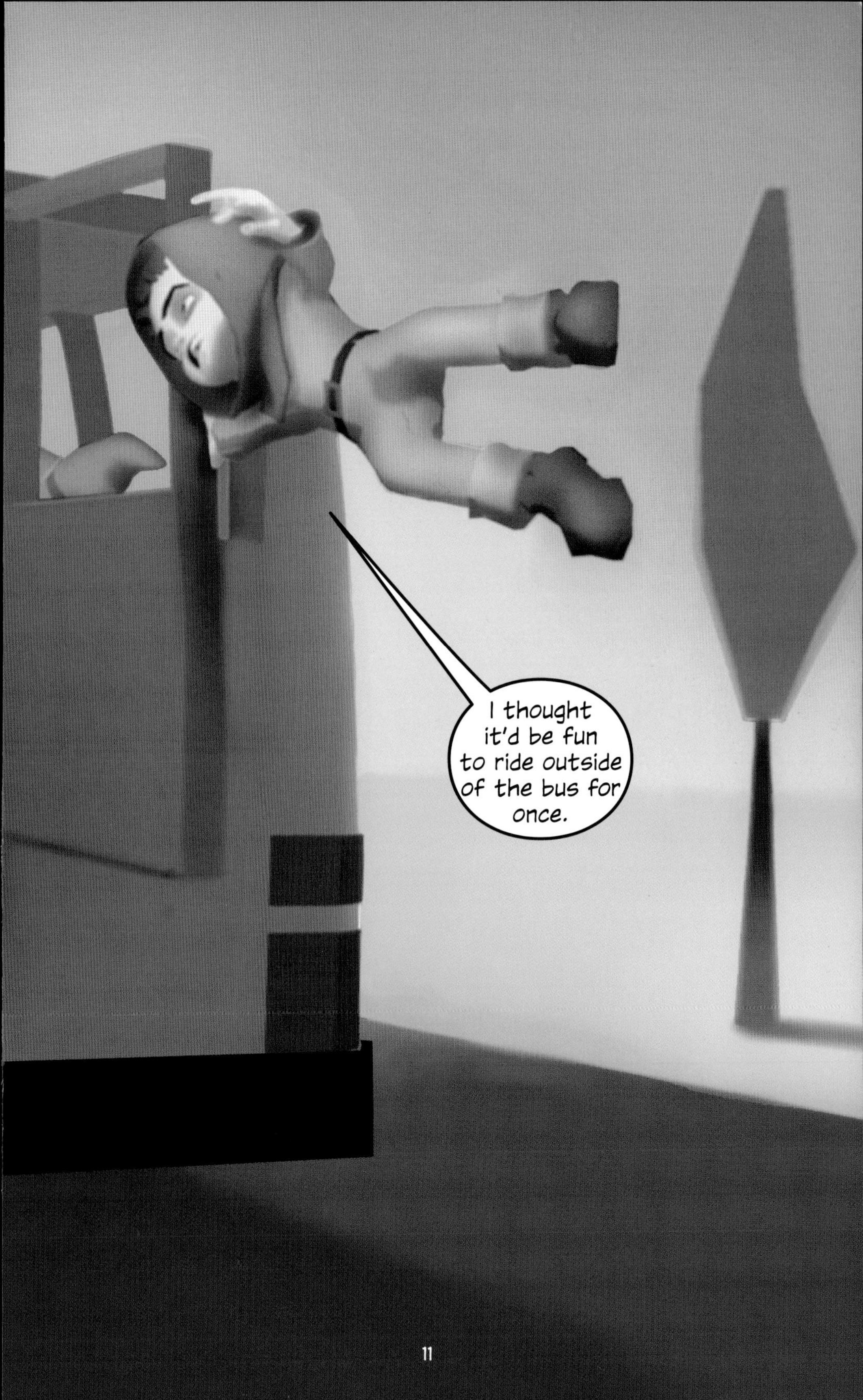
I thought it'd be fun to ride outside of the bus for once.

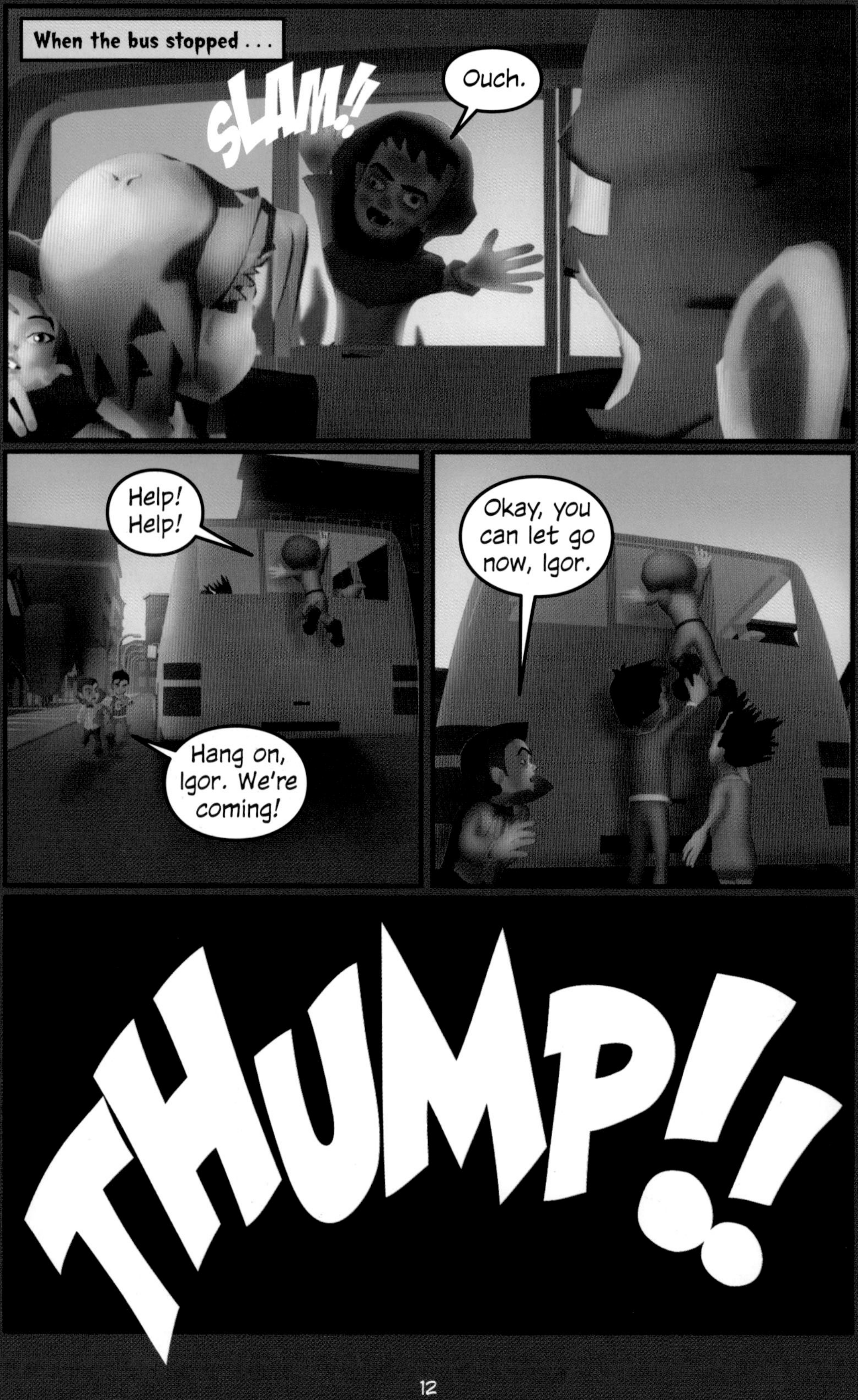
When the bus stopped . . .
SLAM!!
Ouch.
Help! Help!
Hang on, Igor. We're coming!
Okay, you can let go now, Igor.
THUMP!!

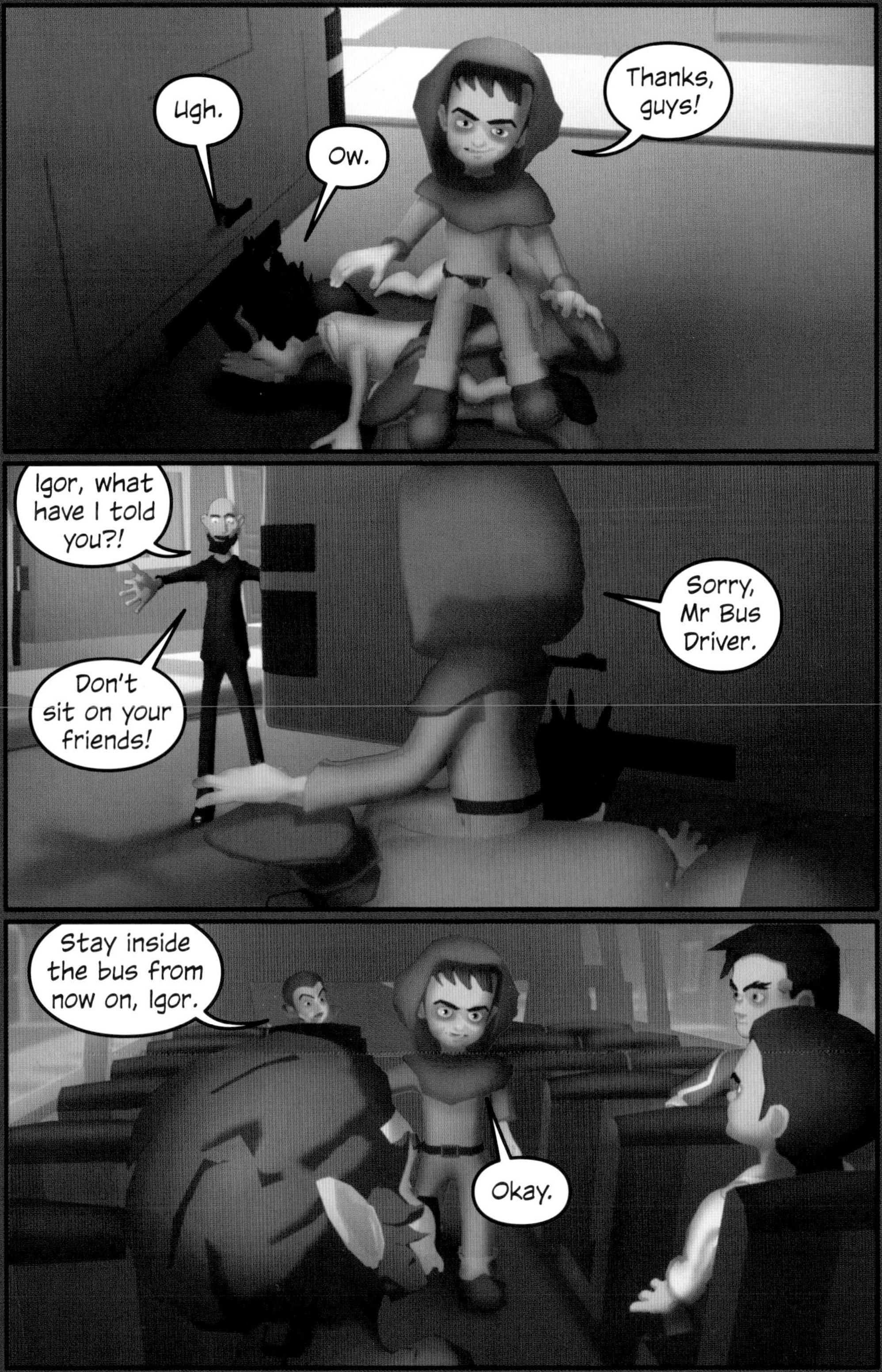
Ugh.
Ow.
Thanks, guys!
Igor, what have I told you?!
Don't sit on your friends!
Sorry, Mr Bus Driver.
Stay inside the bus from now on, Igor.
Okay.

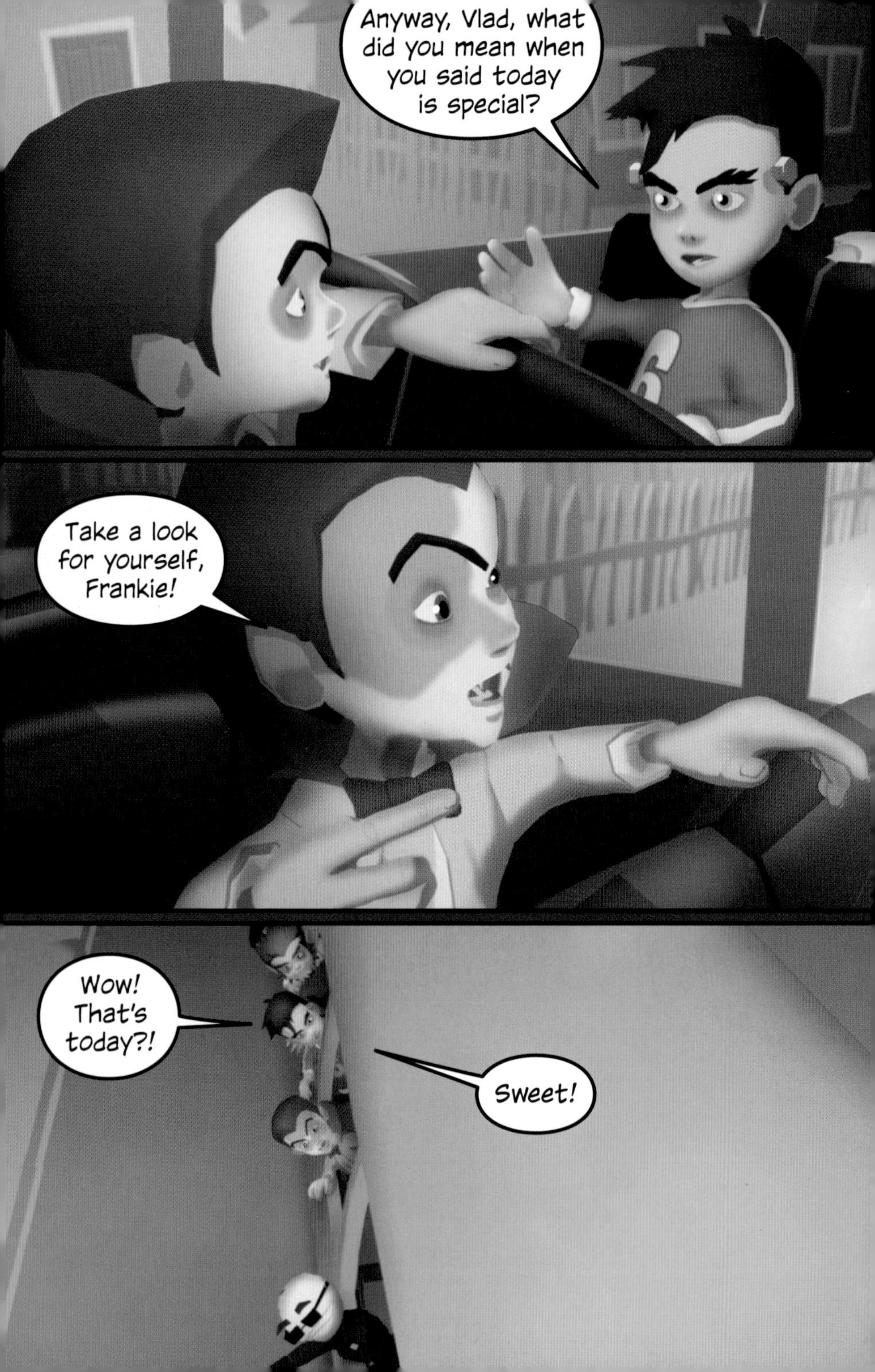
Anyway, Vlad, what did you mean when you said today is special?
Take a look for yourself, Frankie!
Wow! That's today?!
Sweet!

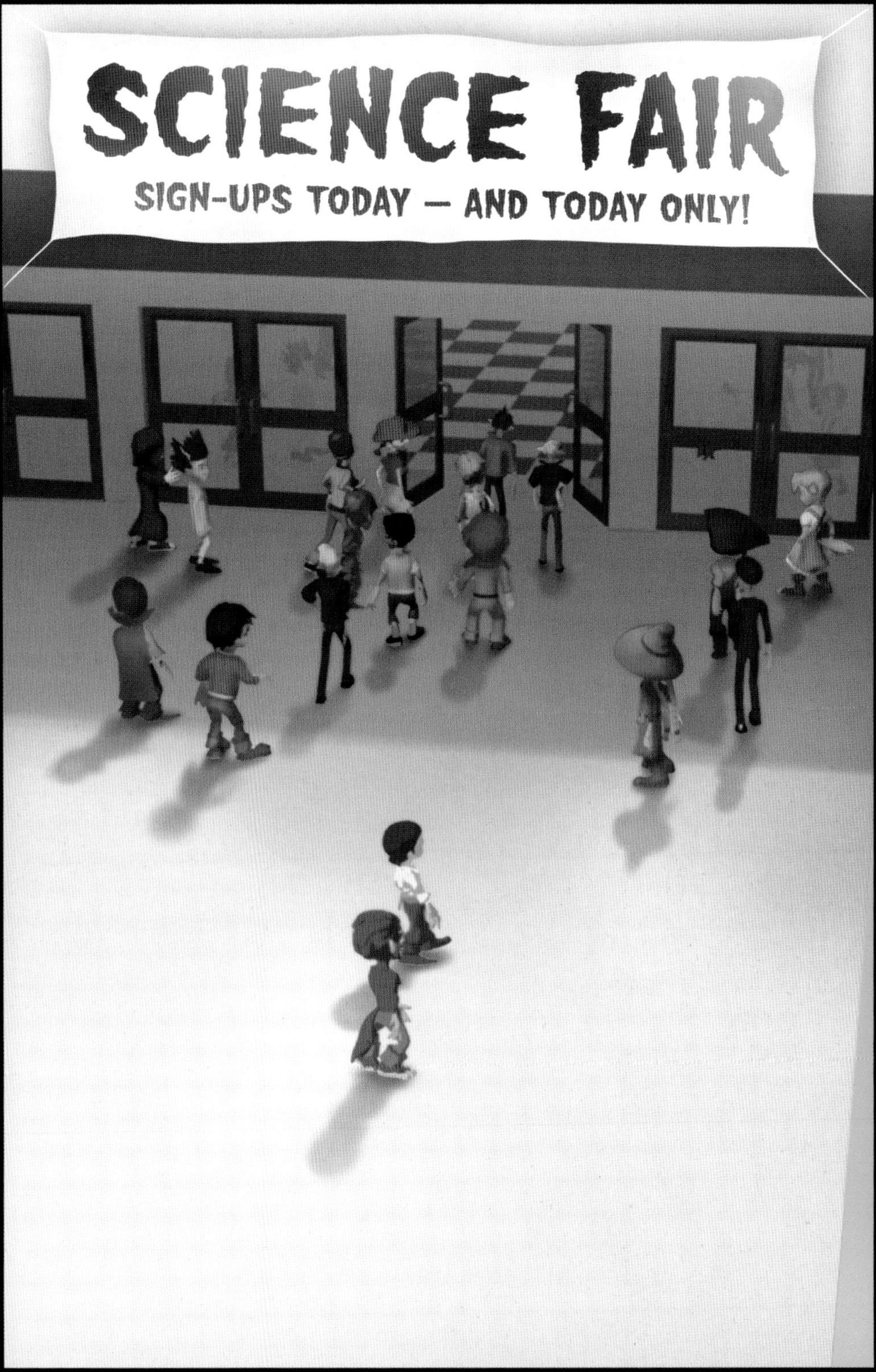
SCIENCE FAIR
SIGN-UPS TODAY – AND TODAY ONLY!

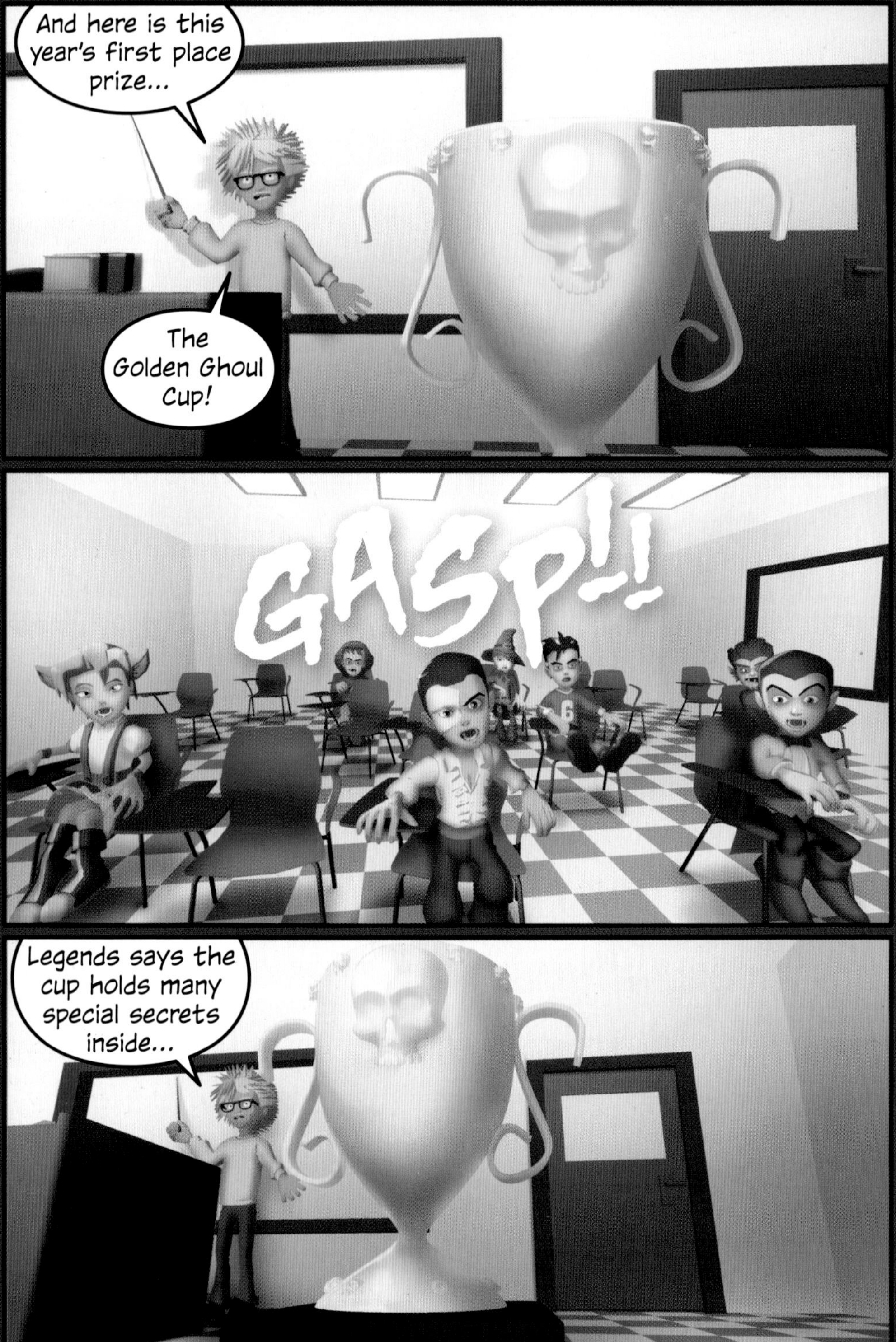
And here is this year's first place prize...
The Golden Ghoul Cup!
GASP!!
Legends says the cup holds many special secrets inside...

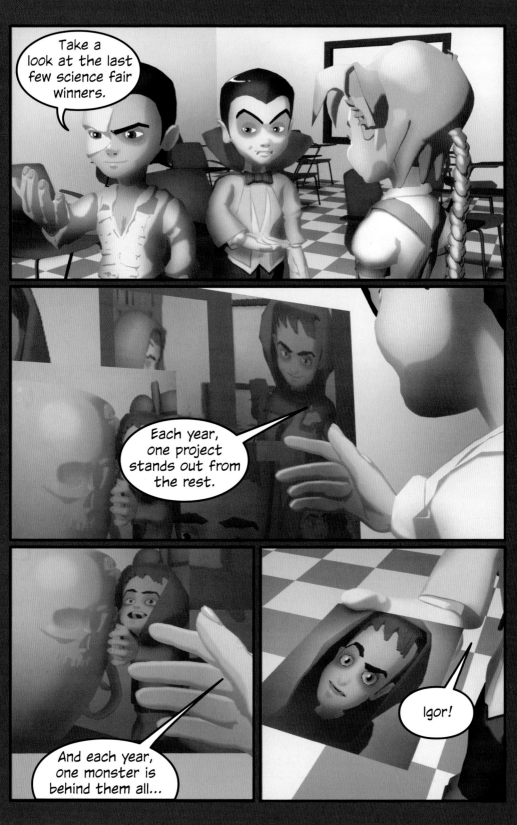

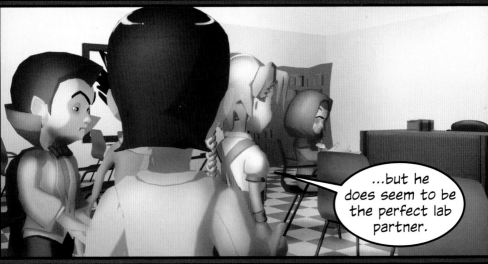

26

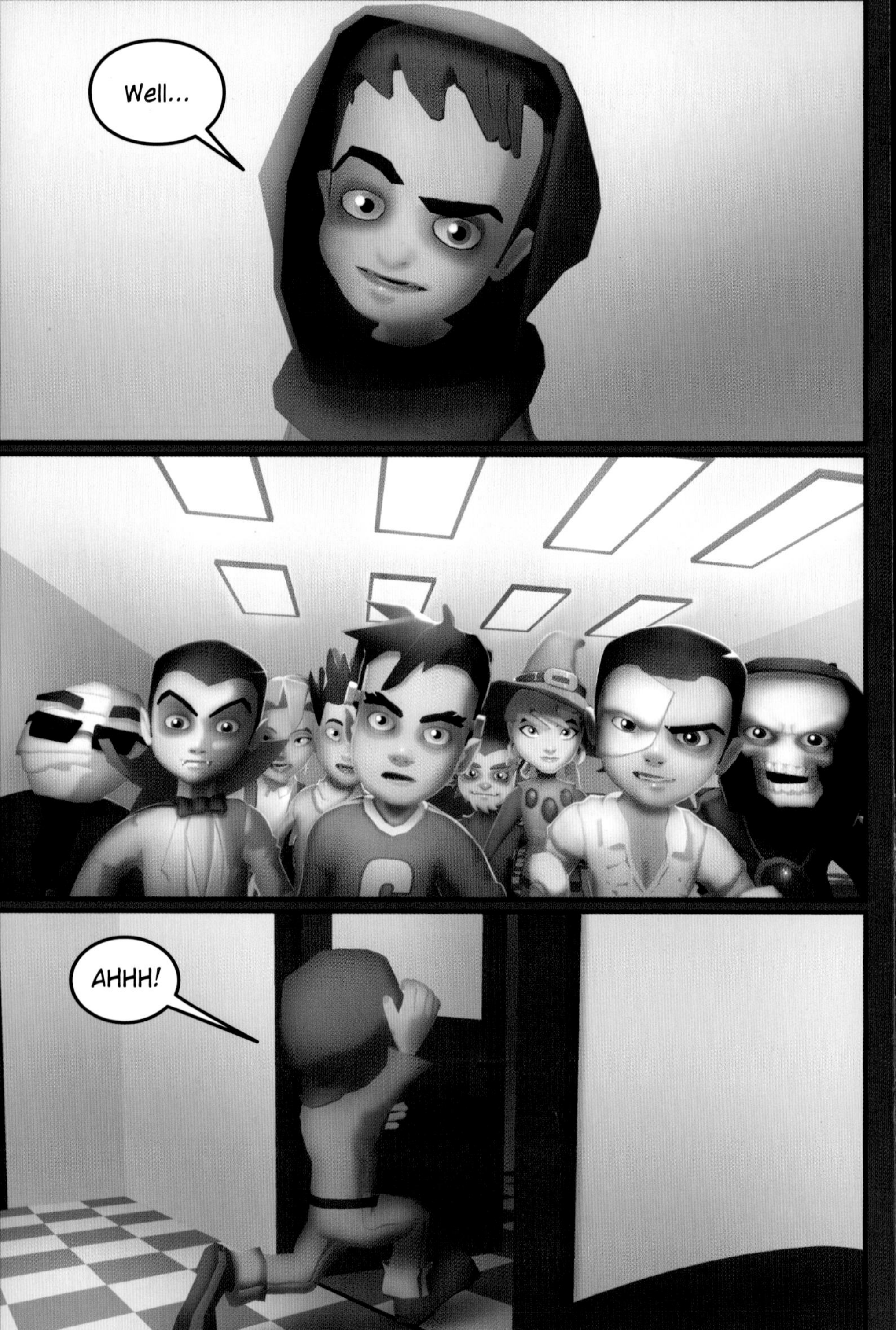
Well...
AHHH!

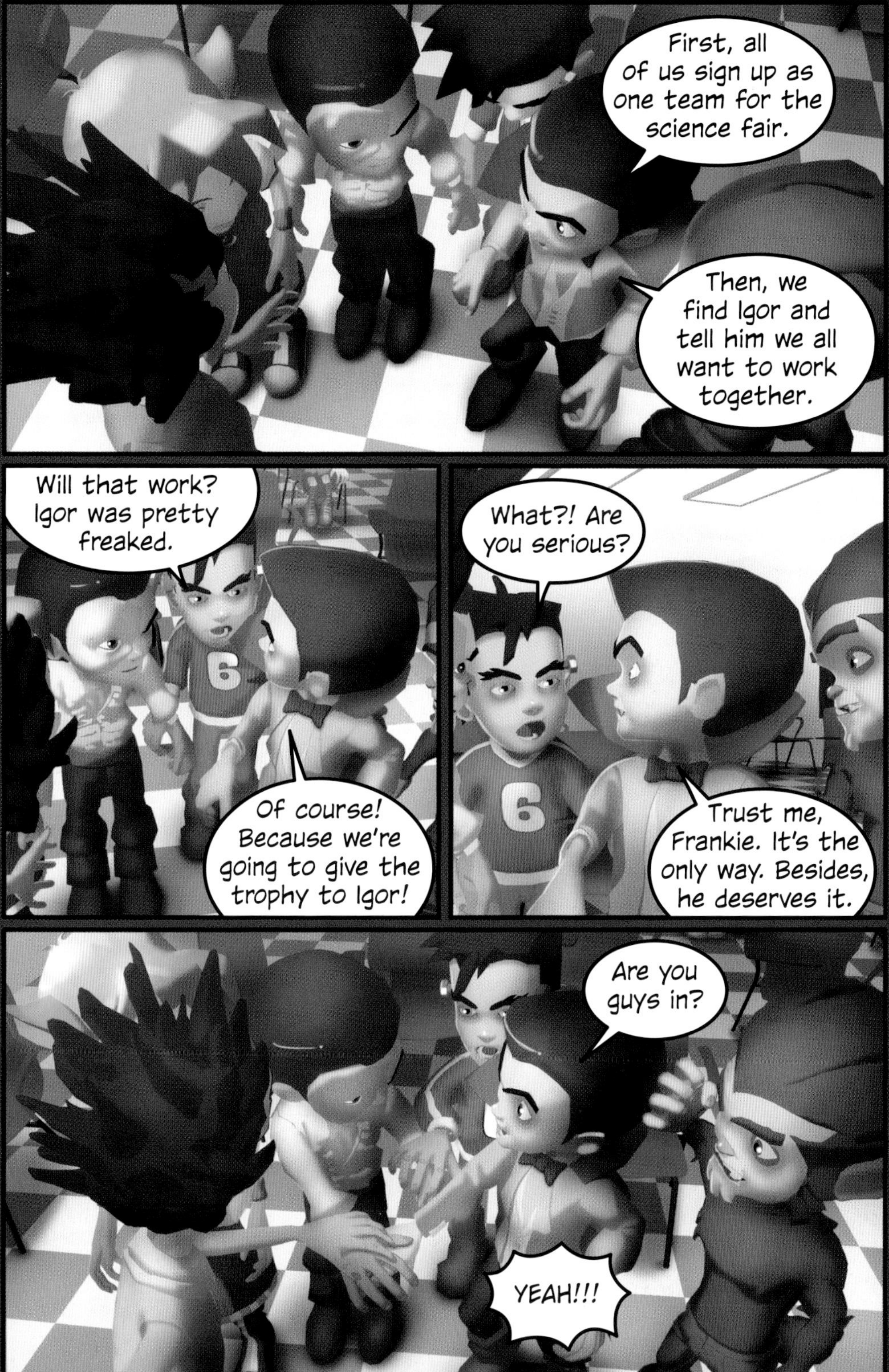
First, all of us sign up as one team for the science fair.
Then, we find Igor and tell him we all want to work together.
Will that work? Igor was pretty freaked.
Of course! Because we're going to give the trophy to Igor!
What?! Are you serious?
Trust me, Frankie. It's the only way. Besides, he deserves it.
Are you guys in?
YEAH!!!

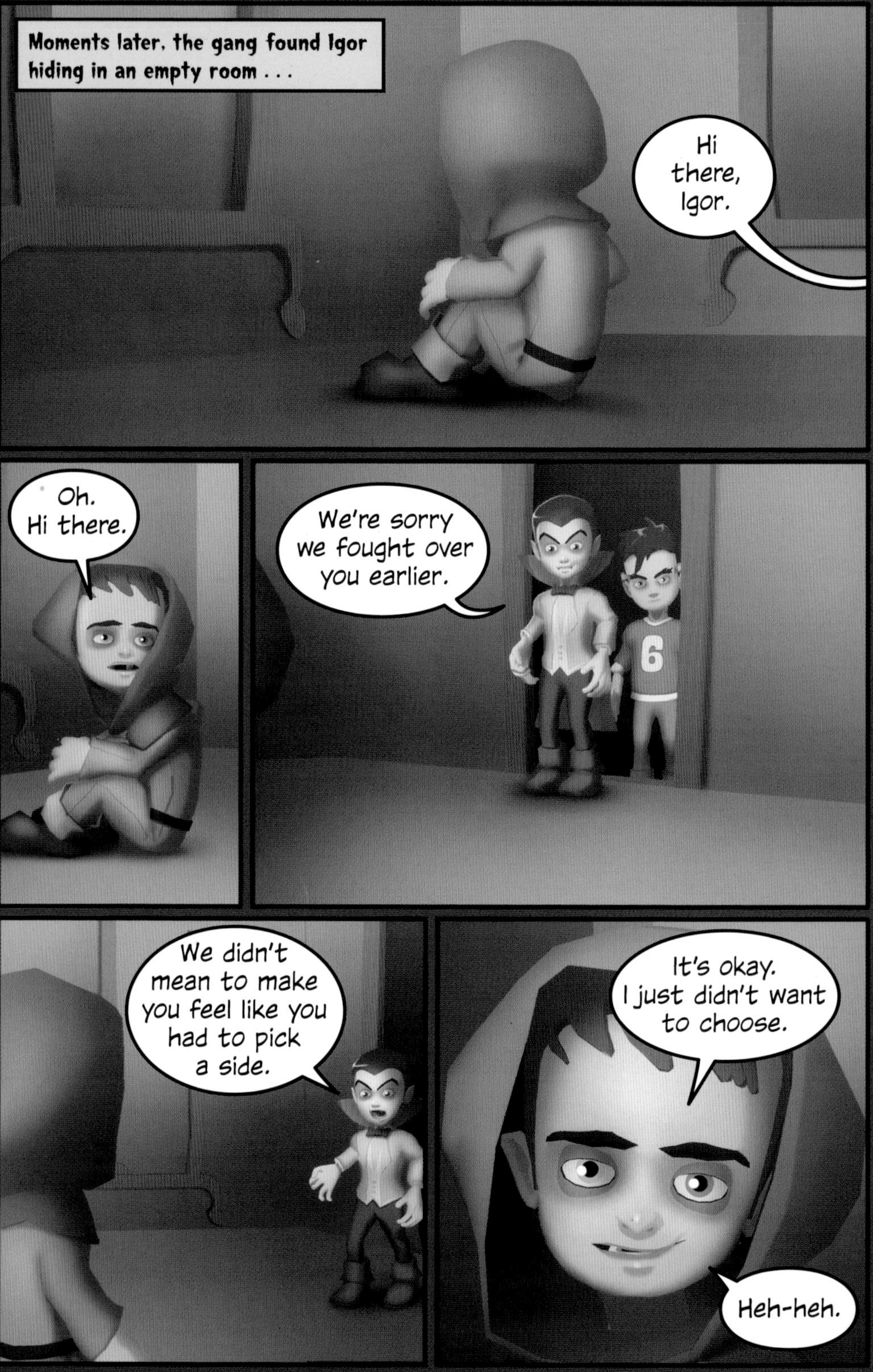
Moments later, the gang found Igor hiding in an empty room . . .
Hi there, Igor.
Oh. Hi there.
We're sorry we fought over you earlier.
6
We didn't mean to make you feel like you had to pick a side.
It's okay. I just didn't want to choose.
Heh-heh.

... while Frankie and Mary put wires in play.

The others teamed up to prepare for some art ...

... while Witchita patiently brewed up her part!

ABOUT
SEAN O'REILLY
AND ARCANA STUDIO

As a lifelong comics fan, Sean O'Reilly dreamed of becoming a comic book creator. In 2004, he realized that dream by creating Arcana Studio. In one short year, O'Reilly took his studio from a one-person operation in his basement to an award-winning comic book publisher with more than 150 graphic novels produced for Harper Collins, Simon & Schuster, Random House, Scholastic and others.

Within a year, the company won many awards including the Shuster Award for Outstanding Publisher and the Moonbeam Award for top children's graphic novel. O'Reilly also won the Top 40 Under 40 award from the city of Vancouver and authored *The Clockwork Girl* for Top Graphic Novel at Book Expo America in 2009. Currently, O'Reilly is one of the most prolific independent comic book writers in Canada. While showing no signs of slowing down in comics, he now writes screenplays and adapts his creations for the big screen.

GLOSSARY

disaster (duh-zah-stuh) – an event that causes great damage, loss or suffering

duet (dyoo-ET) – a piece of music or a song that is performed by two singers

envy (EN-vee) – when you envy someone, you want what that person has

experiment (ek-SPER-uh-ment) – a scientific test to try out a theory or to see the effect of something

forced (FORSSD) – made someone do something

ghoul (GOOL) – an evil creature that feeds on human beings

potions (POE-shuhnz) – a drinkable medicinal or magical liquid

previous (PREE-vee-uhss) – former, or happening before

strategize (STRAT-uh-jize) – if you strategize, you try to create a clever plan to get something done

DISCUSSION QUESTIONS

1. Why did Igor run away screaming from his friends? What do you think bothered him about the situation? Talk about it.

2. The reward for winning the Science Fair is the Golden Ghoul Cup. What kind of prize would you want for winning a contest? Why?

3. Igor's a great lab assistant. What are you good at? Talk about your talents.

WRITING PROMPTS

1. Mr West is the Mighty Mighty Monsters' favourite teacher. Who is your favourite teacher? Why? Write about your favourite teacher.

2. Think up your own science fair experiment. What would your experiment do? What would it prove? Write about your science experiment.

3. If you were one of the Mighty Mighty Monsters, what type of monster would you be? Write a paragraph about your new identity as a monster, then draw a picture of your monstrous self.

Mighty Mighty MONSTERS ADVENTURES

Mighty Mighty MONSTERS
The KING of HALLOWEEN CASTLE
GRAPHIC NOVEL

Mighty Mighty MONSTERS
HIDE and SHRIEK!
GRAPHIC NOVEL

Mighty Mighty MONSTERS
Lost in SPOOKY FOREST
by Sean O'Reilly
GRAPHIC NOVEL

Mighty Mighty MONSTERS
My MISSING MONSTER
by Sean O'Reilly

Mighty Mighty MONSTERS
NEW MONSTER in SCHOOL
by Sean O'Reilly
GRAPHIC NOVEL

Mighty Mighty MONSTERS
MONSTER MANSION
GRAPHIC NOVEL
by Sean O'Reilly

Mighty Mighty MONSTERS
THE MONSTER CROOKS
by Sean O'Reilly
GRAPHIC NOVEL

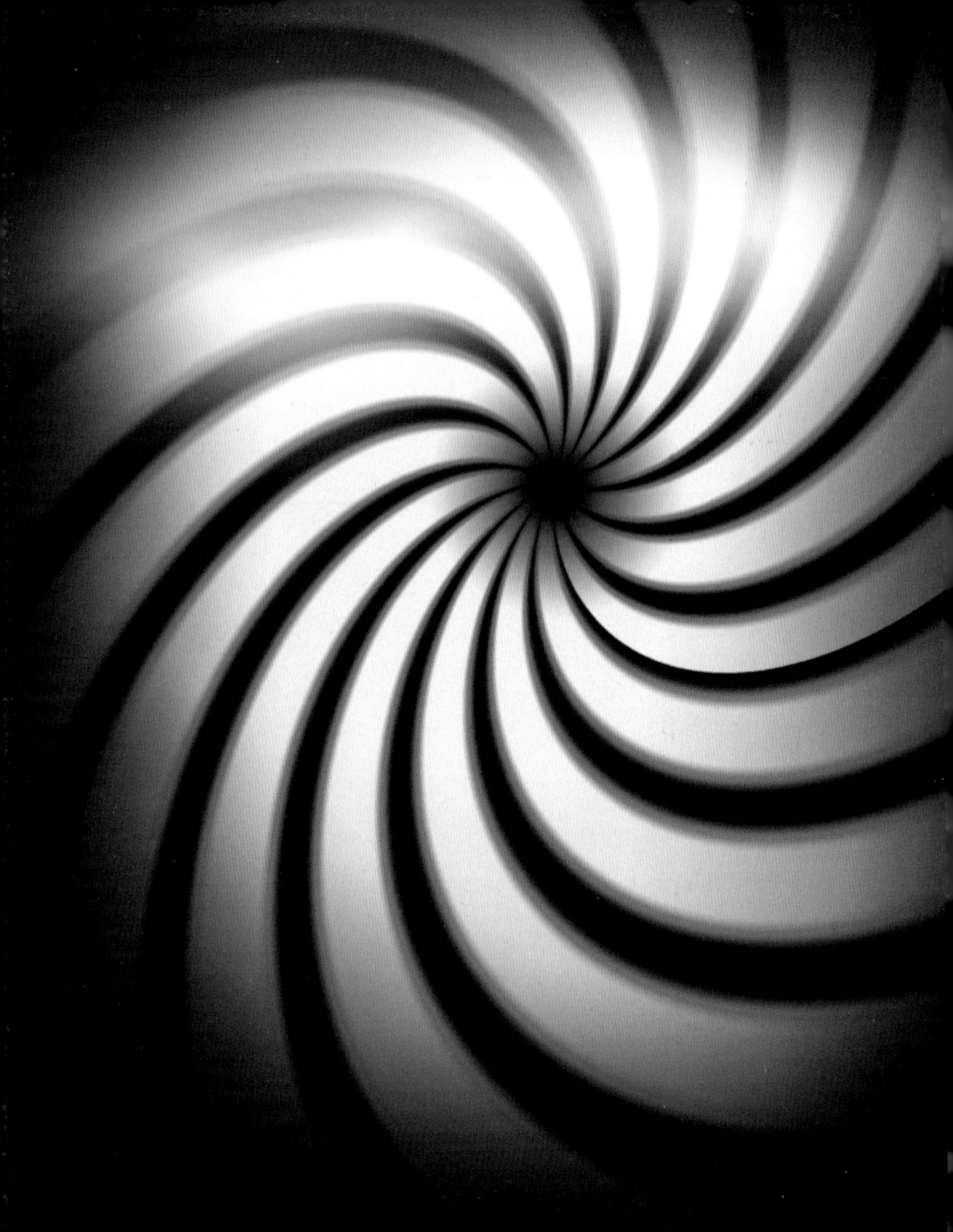

www.raintree.co.uk